A Note to Parents and Caregivers:

Read-it! Readers are for children who are just starting on the amazing road to reading. These beautiful books support both the acquisition of reading skills and the love of books.

 The PURPLE LEVEL presents basic topics and objects using high frequency words and simple language patterns.

 The RED LEVEL presents familiar topics using common words and repeating sentence patterns.

 The BLUE LEVEL presents new ideas using a larger vocabulary and varied sentence structure.

 The YELLOW LEVEL presents more challenging ideas, a broad vocabulary, and wide variety in sentence structure.

 The GREEN LEVEL presents more complex ideas, an extended vocabulary range, and expanded language structures.

 The ORANGE LEVEL presents a wide range of ideas and concepts using challenging vocabulary and complex language structures.

When sharing a book with your child, read in short stretches, pausing often to talk about the pictures. Have your child turn the pages and point to the pictures and familiar words. And be sure to reread favorite stories or parts of stories.

There is no right or wrong way to share books with children. Find time to read with your child, and pass on the legacy of literacy.

Adria F. Klein, Ph.D.
Professor Emeritus
California State University
San Bernardino, California

For my little brother, Mike, and his big, red night-light—J.K.

Editor: Christianne Jones
Designer: Nathan Gassman
Page Production: Angela Kilmer
Creative Director: Keith Griffin
Editorial Director: Carol Jones
The illustrations in this book were created digitally.

Picture Window Books
5115 Excelsior Boulevard
Suite 232
Minneapolis, MN 55416
877-845-8392
www.picturewindowbooks.com

Printed in the United States of America.

Library of Congress Cataloging-in-Publication Data
Kalz, Jill.
Mike's night-light / by Jill Kalz ; illustrated by Thomas Spence.
p. cm. — (Read-it! readers)
Summary: When Mike goes to bed at night, the images that his night-light creates
on the walls of his room stimulate even more images in his mind.
ISBN 1-4048-1726-3 (hardcover)
[1. Imagination—Fiction. 2. Night—Fiction. 3. Bedtime—Fiction.]
I. Spence, Thomas, 1980-, ill. II. Title. III. Series.

PZ7.K12655Mik 2005
[E]—dc22   2005028577

Mike's Night-light

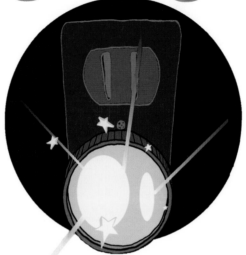

by Jill Kalz
illustrated by Thomas Spence

Special thanks to our advisers for their expertise:

Adria F. Klein, Ph.D.
Professor Emeritus, California State University
San Bernardino, California

Susan Kesselring, M.A.
Literacy Educator
Rosemount–Apple Valley–Eagan (Minnesota) School District

PICTURE WINDOW BOOKS
Minneapolis, Minnesota

Mike sleeps with a night-light.

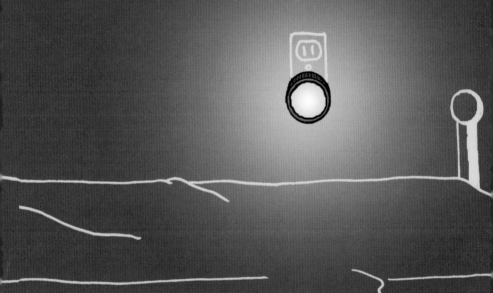

Some nights, the light
looks like a small sun.

Mike sees giraffes and zebras playing under the sun.

Some nights, the light looks like a train.

Mike hears the whistle and rumble
of the train.

Some nights, the light looks like a dentist.

10

Some nights, the light looks like a campfire.

Mike smells marshmallows toasting over the campfire.

13

Tonight, the light twinkles like a star.

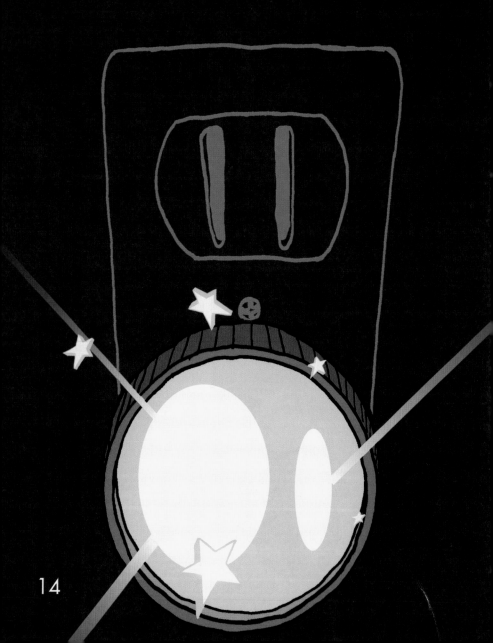

Mike feels like he is
floating in space.

16

Shhh. Mike is asleep.

But in his dreams, the
night-light still glows.

In Mike's dream, a dentist drives
a train filled with zebras.

Giraffes toast marshmallows.
They even make s'mores.

Mike sleeps with a lot of night-lights.
Each one makes him smile.

More *Read-it!* Readers

Bright pictures and fun stories help you practice your reading skills. Look for more books at your level.

At the Beach 1-4048-0651-2
Bears on Ice 1-4048-1577-5
The Bossy Rooster 1-4048-0051-4
Dust Bunnies 1-4048-1168-0
Flying with Oliver 1-4048-1583-X
Frog Pajama Party 1-4048-1170-2
Galen's Camera 1-4048-1610-0
Jack's Party 1-4048-0060-3
The Lifeguard 1-4048-1584-8
Nate the Dinosaur 1-4048-1728-X
The Playground Snake 1-4048-0556-7
Recycled! 1-4048-0068-9
Robin's New Glasses 1-4048-1587-2
The Sassy Monkey 1-4048-0058-1
Tuckerbean 1-4048-1591-0
What's Bugging Pamela? 1-4048-1189-3

Looking for a specific title or level? A complete list of *Read-it!* Readers is available on our Web site:
www.picturewindowbooks.com